THE PLATYPUS ADVENTURES
IN NEW YORK!

LEAH TODD
ILLUSTRATIONS BY LOU DAHL

Leah Todd
The Platypus Adventures In New York
Leah Todd Creative
Copyright 2021 by Leah Todd
First Edition
Print ISBN (Soft cover) 978-1-7776551-0-5
Print ISBN (Hard cover) 978-1-7776551-1-2
eBook (Kindle) ISBN 978-1-7776551-2-9

Book Design & Illustrations | Lou Dahl
Publishing Support | TSPA The Self Publishing Agency, Inc.

DEDICATED TO MY BROTHER
JACKSON (AKA "GORDON"),
WITHOUT WHOM THIS
BOOK WOULDN'T EXIST.

TWO PLATYPUS BROTHERS LIVED
IN THE STEAMY TROPICAL WATERS
OF FAR NORTH QUEENSLAND, AUSTRALIA.

GORDON, THE YOUNGER BROTHER, WAS THE LIFE OF THE PARTY.
HE LOVED SURFING THE RIVER WAVES, CHASING SNAKES,
AND CRACKING JOKES TO ANYONE WHO WOULD LISTEN.

HIS OLDER BROTHER, GOGSWELL, WAS QUIETER AND A LITTLE BIT
MORE SERIOUS, AND ENJOYED STUDYING AND LEARNING.
HE HAD A DEEP CURIOSITY AND RESPECT FOR THE WORLD AROUND HIM.

THE BROTHERS LOVED THEIR LIFE IN AUSTRALIA, BUT THEY HAD GROWN UP HEARING STORIES ABOUT A PLACE CALLED NEW YORK CITY. THERE WERE ENDLESS THINGS FOR A PLATYPUS TO EXPERIENCE THERE, AND GIANT BUILDINGS CALLED SKYSCRAPERS THAT REACHED UP HIGHER THAN BIRDS COULD FLY!

THEY DECIDED TO BOOK THEIR FIRST AIRPLANE TRIP, AND FLY ACROSS THE WORLD TO VISIT NEW YORK CITY TOGETHER.

THEY WERE NERVOUS TO TRAVEL SO FAR FROM HOME, BUT THEIR FAMILY SURROUNDED THEM, SMOTHERING THEM IN HUGS AND KISSES.

"BRING US BACK A SOUVENIR!"

THE FAMILY CRIED, WAVING AND SMILING AS THE TWO BOYS BOARDED THE PLANE.

ON THE PLANE, THEY GOBBLED UP MACARONI AND CHEESE.
THEY WATCHED THREE MOVIES, AND GORDON JUMPED INTO THE
AISLE AND GOT THE WHOLE PLANE LAUGHING,
TELLING STORIES ABOUT ALL OF THE

CRAZY ANIMALS IN AUSTRALIA.

JUST AS THEY WERE DOZING OFF, THE CAPTAIN ANNOUNCED: "NOW ARRIVING INTO NEW YORK CITY!"
THEIR HEADS SNAPPED UP, AND THEY EAGERLY PRESSED THEIR BEAKS AGAINST THE TINY WINDOW,
GAZING IN DISBELIEF AT WHAT THEY SAW BELOW.

GIANT BUILDINGS WERE BUNDLED TOGETHER ON A CONCRETE ISLAND,

AND ALL AROUND THE ISLAND WAS GLITTERING WATER. IN THE MIDDLE OF THE ISLAND WAS A HUGE PARK.
THERE WERE MILLIONS OF CARS LINED UP AND DOWN ALL THE STREETS, AND TWINKLING LIGHTS AS FAR AS THEIR EYES COULD SEE.

A BRIGHT YELLOW TAXI SCREECHED UP TO THEIR HOTEL.
WHEN THE BROTHERS GOT TO THEIR ROOM, THEY THREW THEIR SUITCASES DOWN
AND JUMPED UP AND DOWN ON THEIR BEDS IN EXCITEMENT.

"CAN YOU BELIEVE WE'RE REALLY HERE?" GORDON SAID, HIS EYES BUGGING OUT.

OUTSIDE, THE WORLD WAS BUZZING WITH NEW SOUNDS AND SMELLS.
THE SIDEWALKS WERE CROWDED WITH PEOPLE WALKING QUICKLY IN EVERY DIRECTION,
WAVING AND SHOUTING GREETINGS TO EACH OTHER. THE AIR WAS ELECTRIC,

AND THE DAY SEEMED FULL OF POSSIBILITIES.

GOGSWELL GRINNED AT HIS LITTLE BROTHER. "COME ON, GORDO!
LET'S GO SEE WHAT NEW YORK HAS TO OFFER A COUPLE OF PLATYPUSES!"

THEY PULLED UP TO A CROWD GATHERED AROUND A GROUP OF VIBRANT MEN PLAYING ON STEEL DRUMS. GORDAN AND
GOGSWELL HAD NEVER HEARD THIS TYPE OF MUSIC BEFORE, AND THEY LEAPED INTO THE MIDDLE OF THE CIRCLE,

THEIR WEBBED FEET BOUNCING WILDLY TO THE BEAT.

A TREE-LINED LAKE TWINKLED IN THE AFTERNOON SUN. AFTER THE DANCING THEY NEEDED TO COOL OFF,
SO THEY PLUNGED INTO THE COOL WATER AND SHOWED THE LOCAL DUCKS AND SEAGULLS
HOW TO DO THE "PLATYPUS BACKSTROKE."

GOGSWELL FELT THE URGE TO PAINT AND SKETCH THE PLANTS THAT WERE SO DIFFERENT FROM WHERE
HE GREW UP. GORDON HAD ENERGY TO BURN, SO HE QUICKLY INTRODUCED HIMSELF TO SOME OTHER KIDS
AND JUMPED RIGHT INTO A GAME OF TAG!

THEY WOKE UP THE NEXT MORNING TO BRIGHT SUNSHINE, AND

LEAPT OUT OF BED

TO CATCH THEIR FIRST BASEBALL GAME. THEY BOUGHT NEW YORK YANKEES HATS
AND REAL BASEBALL GLOVES, AND SAT FRONT ROW AT YANKEE STADIUM,
CHEERING ALONG WITH THE BOISTEROUS CROWD.

AT THE SEVENTH INNING STRETCH THEY FELT THEIR BELLIES RUMBLING.
BACK HOME THEY USUALLY ATE BUGS AND LITTLE STREAM FISH, BUT
THE SMELLS FLOATING DOWN FROM THE BUSTLING FOOD STANDS
MADE IT IMPOSSIBLE NOT TO BITE INTO A DELICIOUS,

FULLY LOADED HOT DOG.

"HEY GORDO, YOU'VE GOT SOME MUSTARD ON YOUR BEAK!"
GOGSWELL SHOUTED, DOUBLING OVER WITH LAUGHTER.

THEY SLAPPED THEIR TAILS TOGETHER IN A HIGH FIVE
AS THE YANKEES HIT A HOME RUN RIGHT OUT OF THE PARK!

NEXT STOP WAS TIMES SQUARE,

WHERE THEY GOT THEIR PICTURE TAKEN WITH A GIANT M&M.
THEY STARED UP AT BUILDINGS THAT WERE COVERED TOP TO BOTTOM
WITH FLASHING NEON ADVERTISEMENTS. MASSIVE BILLBOARDS TOWERED
ABOVE THEM AND MUSIC BLASTED FROM EVERY DIRECTION.

THEY BOBBED ALONG WITH THE FRIENDLY CROWDS OF PEOPLE, POPPING
INTO STORES TO SAMPLE FRESH FUDGE AND ICE-COLD LEMONADE, AND
THEY CRANED THEIR NECKS TO TAKE IN THE SEA OF COLOURS
MAKING THEIR EYES SWIM.

TO BRING HOME TO AUSTRALIA, THEY BOUGHT A GIANT STUFFED BEAR
IN A T-SHIRT THAT SAID

I  NY.

WHEN THEY WOKE UP THE NEXT DAY, THERE WAS A COOL MIST OVER THE OCEAN.
THEY TOOK A FERRY TO LIBERTY ISLAND, WHERE THEY GAZED UP IN AMAZEMENT
AT THE TOWERING STATUE OF LIBERTY. THE GIANT GREEN SILHOUETTE
WITH HER ARM OUTSTRETCHED MADE THEM FEEL TINY.

"I NEVER IMAGINED IT WOULD BE THIS BIG,"
WHISPERED GORDON AS HE LEANED INTO HIS BROTHER'S SHOULDER.
"ME EITHER," SAID GOGSWELL AS HE CAREFULLY SNAPPED A PHOTO.

"BUT I'LL NEVER FORGET THIS."

GOGSWELL THOUGHT OF ALL THE PEOPLE WHO HAD STOOD HERE BEFORE HIM
AND FELT THE SAME WAY. IT MADE HIM MISS HIS FAMILY,
AND HE WISHED THEY COULD BE THERE, TOO.

THE LAST DAY OF THE TRIP, THEY WENT

DEEP UNDERGROUND INTO THE NEW YORK SUBWAY.

ALL OVER THE STATION WALLS WAS COLOURFUL GRAFFITI ART, AND A GIRL
STOOD SINGING AT THE TOP OF HER LUNGS WITH A GUITAR CASE IN FRONT OF HER.

ON THE TRAIN, EVERYONE LOOKED DIFFERENT,

AND YET EVERYONE WAS SWAYING TOGETHER TO THE RHYTHM AND HUM OF THE TRAIN.
GORDON GRINNED AND HIGH-FIVED A KID WITH BRIGHT PINK HAIR WHO CAUGHT HIS EYE AND SMILED.
THERE WERE SO MANY PEOPLE ON THE TRAIN, YET IT DIDN'T FEEL STRANGE. IT FELT LIKE FUN.
THEY RODE THE TRAIN FOR HOURS, WATCHING THE PEOPLE COME AND GO.

THEN THEY SAT ON A PARK BENCH LOOKING OVER THE BROOKLYN BRIDGE AT SUNSET,

MUNCHING A DELICIOUS CHEESY NEW YORK PIZZA

AS THE SKY TURNED A DEEP ORANGE.

THE NEXT MORNING
THEY WATCHED THE SCENERY FLY BY
ON THE WAY TO JFK AIRPORT.

AS THEIR PLANE FINALLY BEGAN TO TOUCH DOWN INTO FAR NORTH QUEENSLAND,
THEY ONCE AGAIN PRESSED THEIR BEAKS AGAINST THE LITTLE WINDOW.
THEY SAW THE FAMILIAR DRY RED SOIL, AND THEY SAW EMERALD GREEN MOUNTAINS.

BEYOND THE MOUNTAINS WAS THE RIVER WHERE THEY LIVED WITH THEIR FAMILY.
TOMORROW THEY WOULD WAKE UP AND EAT BREAKFAST, AND HUG THEIR FRIENDS,
AND GO SURFING IN THE HOT SUN. BUT FOR THE LAST FEW MOMENTS BEFORE THE PLANE
TOUCHED DOWN, THEY THOUGHT ABOUT ALL THE UNIQUE EXPERIENCES THEY'D SHARED.

GOGSWELL SAID, "WE DID IT!"

"WE SURE DID," SAID GORDON. THEN HE PULLED SOMETHING OUT OF HIS POCKET AND
SLOWLY UNFOLDED IT. IT WAS A MAP OF THE WORLD. HE WINKED AT HIS BROTHER AND GRINNED.

"WHERE SHOULD WE GO NEXT?"

Manufactured by Amazon.ca
Bolton, ON

24014428R00017